D0922091

MONSTER

by
Walter Dean Myers

Teacher Guide

Written by
Pat Watson

Note

The hardcover edition of this book, published by HarperCollins Publishers, ©1999, was used to prepare this guide. The page references may differ in other editions.

Please note: Parts of this novel deal with sensitive, mature issues. Please assess the appropriateness of this book for the age level and maturity of your students prior to reading and discussing it with your class.

To order, contact your local school supply store, or—

Novel Units, Inc.
P.O. Box 97
Bulverde, TX 78163-0097

Web site: www.educyberstor.com

Table of Contents

Skills and Strategies

Writing
Essay, script, newspaper article, poetry, letter

Comprehension
Cause/effect, predicting

Listening/Speaking
Discussion

Vocabulary
Target words, definitions, application

Across the Curriculum
Art—caricatures, sketch, painting, photography, collage; Drama—monologue, acting Geography; Music; Film

Literary Elements
Characterization, metaphor, theme, plot development, irony, universality, analogy

Thinking
Research, compare/contrast, analysis, critical thinking

Genre: realistic fiction

Setting: Harlem, Manhattan Detention Center and Courthouse, New York City

Point of View: first-person

Themes: fear, self-perception, guilt/innocence

Conflict: person against person; person against self; person against "the system," i.e., jail and the judicial system

Style: Through interweaving journal entries and a self-written movie script of the trial, the narrative creates a unique flow of events and emotions.

Summary

Sixteen-year-old Steve Harmon is in jail, charged with felony murder. He allegedly acted as the lookout for a drugstore robbery in which the owner of the store was killed. The novel begins with a journal entry depicting Steve's fear as he awaits trial. As the trial unfolds, Steve must face soul-searching questions about his "guilt by association" with unsavory characters, his fear of prison, and the pain he inflicts on those he loves. He begins to wonder if he really is the "monster" that the prosecutor calls him. A series of flashbacks and journal entries reveal Steve's experiences in jail, how he became involved with those who perpetrated the crime, his dream of a future in movie-making, and his love and concern for his family. The actual trial is written in a movie script format. The jury finds Steve "not guilty," and the reader is left with unanswered questions and must ultimately judge whether Steve is innocent or guilty.

Honors for *Monster*

Myers was named the first winner of the Michael L. Printz Award for excellence in literature for young adults, January 2000. The Young Adult Library Services Association, a division of American Library Association (ALA), administers the award, which is sponsored by *Booklist* magazine. The award honors the late Michael L. Printz, a school librarian from Topeka, Kansas, who is noted for discovering and promoting quality books for young adults.

Background Information

When asked how he came to write *Monster*, Myers stated that, after leaving school at 16 and spending several years in various jobs, he returned to Empire State College, planning to major in communications. Because of his desire to communicate with people from his own background, a teacher suggested that he interview street people. This pursuit led him to interviews with prisoners, resulting in 600 pages of notes. He discovered emerging patterns in the prisoner interviews and stated, "They all knew why they were in jail; they knew what crimes they had committed or had been accused of committing, but they never seemed to be really sure of the path that had got them there." In addition, he watched the trial of a 17-year-old boy charged with armed robbery and attempted murder. When asked why he has Steve Harmon tell his story in both personal journal and film script, Myers replied, "I did that because I saw that the prisoners I interviewed were separating their actions, their crimes, from who they were as people." In the novel, Steve writes personal journal entries about his jail experiences and who he really is. He writes about the trial in movie script format because he sees that as apart from his real self.

About the Author

Personal Information: Walter Dean Myers was born August 12, 1937, in Martinsburg, West Virginia, to George and Mary Myers. Herbert and Florence Dean adopted him when he was three years old. The family lived in the Harlem district of New York City. He is married to Constance Brendel and has three children: Karen and Michael Dean from a first marriage, and Christopher from his second marriage. He served in the Army from 1954-1957 and later received a B.A. degree from Empire State College. In addition to his writing career, he has worked as an employment supervisor, a trade book editor, and a teacher of creative writing and Black History. He is a member of PEN and the Harlem Writers Guild. Although perhaps most well known for writing novels that examine the lives of young Black people, Myers also writes skillfully in other mediums such as fantasy and adventure. This versatile author has been writing for more than 30 years.

Writing Career: He began writing poems and stories as a teenager, winning awards for his achievements, but his race and economic status seemed to limit him. However, he continued to write while serving in the U.S. Army and later working at menial jobs and began to have some of his works published in magazines. Winning a contest for picture book writers with his text for *Where Does the Day Go?* inspired him to continue, and writing has been his full-time profession since 1977. A sampling of his numerous works includes *Hoops* (1983), *Motown and Didi* (1987), *Fallen Angels* (1988), *Scorpions* (1990), *The Young Landlords* (1991), *Brown Angels: an Album of Pictures and Verse* (1993), *The Glory Field* (1995), *Harlem* (1997), *Amistad: A Long Road to Freedom* (1998), *At Her Majesty's Request: An African Princess in Victorian England* (1999).

Honors: Five-time winner of the Coretta Scott King Award: *The Young Landlords* (1980), *Motown and Didi* (1985), *Fallen Angels* (1989), *Now Is Your Time! The African-American Struggle for Freedom* (1992) *Slam!* (1997); Newbery Honor Award: *Somewhere in the Darkness, Scorpions*. He received the first Virginia Hamilton Literary Award, the *Boston Globe-Horn Book* award, ALA Margaret A. Edwards Award, New York Council on Interracial Books for Children Award, and numerous notable and best book citations from the ALA.

Characters

Steve Harmon: narrator; 16-year-old protagonist; on trial for felony murder

Kathy O'Brien: Steve's defense attorney

Sandra Petrocelli: prosecutor

Briggs: attorney for King

James King: the "Thug"; one of the perpetrators of the crime

Richard "Bobo" Evans: the "Rat"; one of the perpetrators of the crime

Osvaldo Cruz: member of the Diablos; participant in the crime

Lorelle Henry: eyewitness who places King at the crime scene just prior to the murder

José Delgado: store employee who found the body

Judge: 60 years old; appears bored at beginning of trial

Zinzi and Bolden: prisoners who testify against defendants as part of plea-bargain

Steve's family: his parents and brother Jerry

Mr. Sawicki: Steve's mentor in the film club; testifies in his defense

Court Officials: Det. Karyl (investigating officer), Forbes (city clerk), Moody (medical examiner)

Witnesses for King: Dorothy Moore, George Nipping

Initiating Activities

Use one or more of the following activities to introduce the novel.

1. Place the word "monster" in a circle on an overhead transparency. Have students brainstorm word associations: definitions, visualization, emotions, etc. Look up the word in the dictionary and discuss its various definitions.

2. Place the following quote on the board. Elicit student verbal or written response. "What a chimera then is man! What a novelty! What a monster, what a chaos, what a contradiction, what a prodigy! Judge of all things, feeble earthworm, depository of truth, a sink of uncertainty and error, the glory and the same of the universe...Self is hateful." Blaise Pascal. *Pensees*, #434, #455 (1670).

3. Read the first journal entry (pp. 1-5) aloud. Discuss why the narrator might be in jail and his reaction. Have students complete the following: "Fear is..."

Additional Information

Poetry

Name Poem: Write the person's name vertically on paper. Use the letters for the first letter of each line. On each line, include one or more adjectives and/or sentences about the person.

Five-senses:

Line 1: color of the emotion

Line 2: sound of the emotion

Line 3: taste of the emotion

Line 4: smell of the emotion

Line 5: sight (what the emotion looks like)

Line 6: feeling evoked by the emotion

Diamente: seven-line contrast poem set up to appear in a diamond shape on paper; contrast in thought occurs in line 4.

Line 1: one word (a noun, the subject)

Line 2: two words (adjectives describing line 1)

Line 3: three words ("ing" or "ed" words that relate to line 1)

Line 4: four words (first two nouns relate to line 1; second two nouns to line 7)

Line 5: three words ("ing" or "ed" words that relate to line 7)

Line 6: two words (adjectives describing line 7)

Line 7: one word (noun that is the opposite of line 1)

Metaphor/Simile Poem:

Line 1: noun (title)

Lines 2-4: write something about the subject; each line should say something different and give an idea of what the subject is like.

Line 5: a metaphor or simile that begins with the title

Sociogram

Directions: Write the name of a different character from *Monster* in each circle. On the "spokes" surrounding each character's name, write several adjectives that describe that character. On the arrows joining one character to another, write a description of the relationship between the two characters. How does one character influence the other?

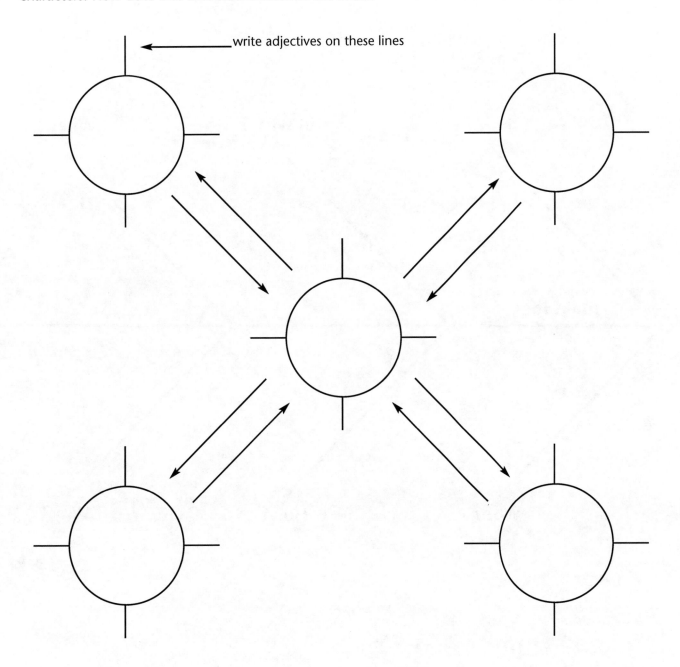

write adjectives on these lines

Herringbone

Directions: Using the novel and your imagination, record the answers to the questions on the herringbone form below. (Who was involved? What did these persons do? When did it happen? Where did it happen? How did it happen? Why did it happen?) Add spaces if there are more than two answers to a question. Then write a newspaper article about the incident.

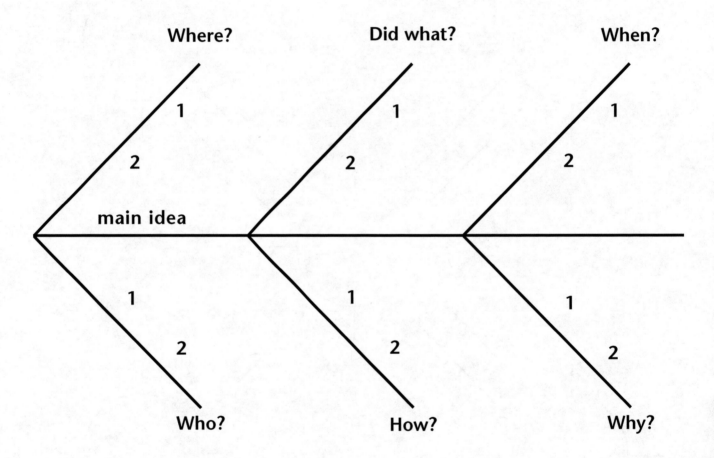

Thematic Analysis

Directions: Choose a theme from the book to be the focus of your word map. Complete a web and then answer the question in each starred box.

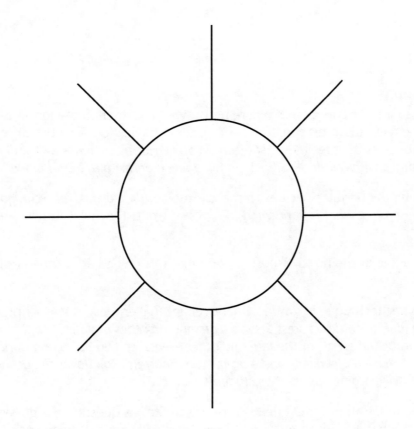

 What is the author's
main message?

 What did you learn
from the book?

9

Pages 1-19

The narrator, Steve Harmon, is in jail feeling alone and frustrated. He decides to write a movie, *Monster*, about his experience. The first courtroom scene introduces other primary characters: O'Brien, Steve's attorney; Petrocelli, the prosecutor; and James King, the man with whom Steve is on trial.

Vocabulary

dispensary (2)   grainy (3)   obscene (7)   felony (12)   mentor (19)

Discussion Questions

1. Identify the narrator and discuss where he is, why he is there, how long he has been there, and how he feels about his situation. Ask students to vicariously put themselves in Steve's place and express their feelings. *(16-year-old Steve Harmon; in jail—Manhattan Detention Center; charged with murder; has been in jail a few months; afraid and alone. pp. 1-5)*

2. Examine why the narrator decides to make a movie. *(It is a survival technique. He is trying to make some sense of what is happening to him and wants the movie to tell of his experience. pp. 4-5)*

3. Analyze the title of the novel, *Monster*, and what this reveals about the crime. *(Responses will vary.)*

4. Discuss Myers' technique in writing the novel: journal entries, movie script, purpose of Voice Over. *(The journal entries express Steve's fears and anxieties and his hatred of jail. The movie script reveals actual events at the trial and other events leading up to and during the trial. Voice Over is a filmmaking technique where an offscreen narrator talks over the action. Additional information will become apparent as students read the novel.)*

5. Analyze the implications of O'Brien's response to Steve's question about winning, "It probably depends on what you mean by 'win.'" *(Responses will vary but should include possibilities of acquittal, degree of punishment, if convicted, etc. p. 13)*

6. Discuss the significance of the cut to the high-school film workshop. *(This introduces Mr. Sawicki, the film club mentor, and reflects another side of Steve Harmon. Sawicki also discusses film techniques and predictable endings. pp. 18-19)*

Supplementary Activities

1. Have students stage the opening scenes of the movie, including the selection of appropriate music and lighting.

2. Have students research the penalty for felony murder and the status of capital punishment in the state in which they live.

3. Ask a student volunteer to sketch his or her impression of Steve Harmon, either in jail or in court.

4. Have students define the film terms used in Steve's script such as VO, CUT TO, CU, and others.

Pages 20-43

The prosecutor's opening statements allege that King and Evans actually perpetrated the crime of robbery and that the owner of the store was killed. Two others were allegedly involved, including Steve Harmon, who acted as the lookout. A jail inmate, Sal Zinzi, presents incriminating testimony.

Vocabulary

safeguard (21)	merits (21)	infringing (21)	conspiracy (23)
impede (23)	redress (26)	lynch (26)	grandiose (27)
articulate (28)	inventory (31)	careens (42)	tentative (42)

Discussion Questions

1. Examine the opening statements of the two attorneys. Ask students if they think an attorney must believe in his or her client in order to conduct an effective defense. *(In Petrocelli's opening statements, she identifies the crime as a felony murder committed during a robbery and alludes to "monsters" in the community who disregard the rights of others. James King and Richard "Bobo" Evans have been accused of the actual murder. She alleges that Steve Harmon acted as the lookout and is, therefore, guilty of the same crime. O'Brien casts doubt on the credibility of the State's key witnesses. Both attorneys are adamant that their "side" is the right one. pp. 20-28)*

2. Discuss the importance of cigarettes to the prosecution and Zinzi's reason for informing. *(The clerk's inventory after the robbery/murder showed 5 cartons of cigarettes missing. Zinzi, witness for the prosecution, tells the court that, while he was incarcerated on Riker's Island, another inmate, Bolden, told him he had bought stolen cigarettes from a man involved in the drugstore robbery. This sets the stage for the implication of Bobo Evans in the crime. Zinzi has become an informer because he is afraid of being gang-raped and wants out of prison. pp. 29-37)*

3. Examine how both Briggs and O'Brien cast doubt on Zinzi's testimony. *(They question his credibility by pointing out that his fear would have caused him to do anything, including lie, to get out of prison. pp. 36-40)*

4. Analyze the purpose of Steve's flashback. *(It reveals how easily an innocent act can lead to trouble. Steve, does not verbalize responsibility for his actions. p. 41)*

Supplementary Activities

1. Select two students the day prior to reading this section. Ask them to be prepared to read the opening statements of the two attorneys. Ask students to write the name of the attorney they think presents the most convincing opening statement.

2. Ask students to read numbers 5, 6, and 8 of the Bill of Rights Amendments to the United States Constitution and be prepared to discuss these as they read the script of Steve's trial.

Pages 45-58

Steve's journal entry reflects on his hatred and fear of jail. The prosecution presents more incriminating testimony.

Vocabulary

drawl (50)   pertinent (55)   silhouetted (57)

Discussion Questions

1. Characterize Bolden by noting the crimes he has committed. Discuss the impact of his testimony. Ask students to analyze how they would feel if he were testifying either for or against them. *(He has been arrested for breaking and entering, possession of drugs with intent to sell, and assault. He says that Bobo Evans sold him cigarettes and told him he got them during a drugstore robbery. pp. 47-49, 52-55)*

2. Examine the purposes of the flashbacks on pages 49-51 and page 58. *(establishes acquaintance of King and Steve and alludes to robbing a drugstore; reveals facts about Steve's home life, including a clean, neatly furnished house and a good relationship with his younger brother, Jerry; shows Steve as a person outside of the courtroom.)*

Supplementary Activities

1. Place Bolden's statement, "I just wanted to do the right thing. You know, like a good citizen." on the board. Analyze the irony of his statement as it compares with his actions. Have students complete the statement, "Being a good citizen means..."

2. Ask for a student volunteer to sketch the courtroom scene.

Pages 59-88

More details about the murder scene unfold. Steve expresses feelings of "nothingness" in jail. Testimony continues to incriminate Steve.

Vocabulary

affidavit (66)	pans (67)	grotesque (68)	pessimist (73)
lethal (73)	grimaces (73)	perpetrator (74)	proposition (85)
juvenile (86)	civil (88)		

Discussion Questions

1. Examine Steve's "loss of identity" while in jail. *(taking away shoelaces and belt, feelings of separation from real self in courtroom and of being one of many in jail, feeling that everyone looks the same, feeling of being less than human, dreams where no one hears or answers him all make him feel that he is nothing. pp. 59-64)*

2. Analyze Steve's flashback of his interrogation by Detectives Karyl and Williams. *(Karyl accuses Steve of the murder; Steve denies any part in the robbery. The conversation between the two detectives, as they discuss the death penalty, is designed to manipulate Steve into a confession. Steve, filled with fear, imagines himself on death row as they prepare him for a lethal injection. pp. 71-73)*

3. Discuss the rationale of the older prisoner when Steve proclaims his innocence. *(He believes Steve is guilty, but even if he is innocent, somebody has to do some time in prison to pay for the crime. pp. 76-77)*

4. Discuss why O'Brien says the trial could be going better and what she believes they must do. *(Nothing is happening to prove Steve's innocence. She thinks half the jurors believed he was guilty when they first saw him because he is young, Black, and on trial. They must show that the prosecutor is not lying but is mistaken. pp. 78-79)*

5. Contrast Steve's flashback of Osvaldo Cruz with Cruz's appearance in court. Discuss the impact of Cruz's testimony. *(Flashback: Cruz acts tough and taunts Steve; Freddy advises Steve to leave him alone because he hangs out with "bad dudes." Courtroom: speaks softly and timidly; says he went along with plans for the robbery because he was afraid of Bobo, James King, and Steve Harmon. pp. 80-87)*

Supplementary Activities

1. Place the maxim "innocent until proven guilty" on the board. Discuss whether or not students think this is true.

2. Read the cliché, "If you run with dogs, you'll get fleas." Have students associate this with Steve's predicament.

3. Have a student draw a caricature of Cruz based on his description on page 80.

Pages 89-113

Steve is tormented by thoughts of a prison term, his home, and Mr. Nesbitt's death. Osvaldo Cruz testifies against Bobo and Steve. O'Brien's cross-examination discredits Cruz. Steve's visit with his father provides the emotional ending for this section.

Vocabulary

judicial (97)   apprehended (102)   ruffled (107)   hexagon (110)
cope (111)

Discussion Questions

1. Analyze Steve's journal entry. *(Steve is discouraged because O'Brien feels the case is not going well. Hearing the prisoners discuss their crimes and jail sentences causes him to reflect on the possibility of his own jail term. The guards' taunts torment him, and the death photos of Nesbitt haunt him. Fear overshadows all other images. pp. 89-98)*

2. Analyze the effect of the Black juror on Steve. How does O'Brien respond to Steve's crying? *(The juror is smiling but stops and quickly looks away when Steve smiles at her. Steve cries and puts his head down on the table. O'Brien angrily tells him to get his head up because that implies he is giving up and will influence the jury. p. 99)*

3. Characterize Osvaldo Cruz by his testimony and appearance in court. What does *Diablos* mean? *(devils; Cruz is two-faced, has made a deal with the government, and will do anything to better himself. He got a girl other than his girlfriend pregnant and he lies about being a member of the Diablos. He admits that he cut a stranger in the face in order to be a member of the gang. pp. 102-109)*

4. Discuss whether or not Steve's dad believes in his innocence. *(With tears in his eyes and pain in his face, Mr. Harmon tells Steve about his dream for Steve's future. He wants to believe that Steve is innocent but shows deep concern as he tries to convince both himself and Steve that everything will be okay. The scene ends with the sound of Mr. Harmon sobbing. pp. 110-113)*

Supplementary Activities

1. Introduce the literary term **universality**. Note the universality of parents' dreams for their children and the effect of children's problems on their parents. *(Responses will vary. pp. 111-113)*

2. Note the slang phrases: holding pen (94), let him walk (95), cutting a deal (96), up to your neck (103).

3. Analyze Mr. Harmon's analogy of the courtroom to a garbage disposal or sewer (p. 110).

Pages 115-126

The scene of Steve's neighborhood reveals his reaction when he heard about the arrest of Bobo Evans and the effect on Steve's mother and brother when Steve was arrested.

Vocabulary

cacophony (117)   ghetto (120)   dismay (121)   glowers (123)
precinct (124)

Discussion Questions

1. Have students reflect on Steve's reaction to causing his father pain. *(Seeing his father cry with such deep emotional grief makes Steve feel terrible and makes him afraid his father sees him as a monster just like all the "bad guys." pp. 115-116)*

2. Discuss whether or not students think Steve is guilty. Note his reference to walking in a drugstore and looking around (p. 115), his reaction when he overhears the women talking about the crime (pp. 117-120), his shock when he hears the report on TV (pp. 120-121), and his stupor after hearing of Bobo's arrest (p. 123). *(Responses will vary. Point out his self-avowed "I didn't do nothing"; his running from the women; his absolute shock.)*

3. Examine the reaction of his mother and his brother when Steve is arrested. Ask students how members of their family would react in a similar situation. Refer also to his father's reaction (question #1). *(His mother panics and tries to follow him, and his brother reaches out to him as the detectives hustle him out the door. pp. 124-126)*

Supplementary Activities

1. Have students bring to class pictures of neighborhoods similar to Steve's (p. 117) and/or pictures and articles relating to Mayor Rudy Giuliani's crackdown on crime in New York City (p. 122).

2. Pinpoint Steve's neighborhood and location of the drugstore on a New York City map. Note key points: Malcolm X Blvd. (p. 48), 141st St. (p. 49), 144th St. (p. 84), Harlem (p. 120).

Pages 127-151

Steve's journal reveals that he joined the others because he wanted to be tough like them. The trial testimony tells how Nesbitt died. Steve struggles with the definition of guilt. His mother visits him in jail.

Vocabulary

arcs (130)	montage (131)	premises (131)	perimeter (133)
traversed (135)	trapezius (135)	wrenched (147)	mosaic (151)

Discussion Questions

1. Discuss Petrocelli's "cheap trick" and whether or not students consider this a convincing technique. *(She shows the jurors death-scene pictures of Nesbitt just before court dismisses for the weekend. She wants the jurors to remember the bad images over the weekend. pp. 127-128)*

2. Examine Steve's reason for being involved in the robbery. Ask students how they feel about the desire of many students to be like someone else and the lengths to which these students will go in order to conform. *(He wanted to be tough like the others. p. 130)*

3. Discuss what the book reveals about Nesbitt and how he died. *(He was a middle-aged Black male. He was dead when detectives arrived at the crime scene. The bullet traveled through his lung and esophagus, causing internal bleeding. He drowned in his own blood. pp. 132-136)*

4. Analyze the two views of "guilt" as portrayed by Steve and Ernie. *(In a journal entry, Steve says he just walked into a drugstore looking for mints, then walked back out, and that he didn't kill Mr. Nesbitt. Ernie acknowledges that he stole money and jewelry but says he isn't guilty because he couldn't get out of the store with the stolen goods. pp. 140-142)*

5. Discuss Steve's mother's visit to him in jail and how she reflects the universality of a mother's love. Ask students how their parents would react in a similar situation. *(Her tears make Steve realize the terrible effect his being in jail has on her. They talk of mundane things. She questions whether or not she should have gotten him a Black lawyer, tells him she will bring Jerry the next day and brings him a Bible. Universality: Steve's mother vows her belief in his innocence and her unconditional love. pp. 144-148)*

6. Read aloud the scripture Steve's mother marks in the Bible she brings him (Psalm 28:7), and ask why she chooses that particular verse. Note and discuss key words: "strength," "shield," "trust," "help," "rejoice," "praise." (*Responses will vary but should include cause/effect: If God is the strength and shield, people can trust in Him and find help, then rejoice and praise Him. p. 146*)

Supplementary Activities

1. Have students write a letter from Steve's mother to a relative expressing how she feels after visiting him in jail, how she views his chance for acquittal, and how his imprisonment is affecting the family.

2. Analyze the metaphor, "I [Steve] can see me at that moment, just when Mr. Nesbitt knew he was going to die, walking down the street trying to make my mind a blank screen" (p. 128).

3. Have students interpret the slang: packing it in (p. 132), chalked the body (p. 133), have done a whole calendar (p. 147), smokes a joint (149), put together a payroll crew (p. 149), no badges copping some z's (p. 150).

Pages 153-171

Steve's journal tells of the tedium of jail life and the unreality of his family visits. A witness for the prosecution identifies King as one of the two men who argued with Nesbitt the day of the murder.

Vocabulary

whist (154)   diminutive (161)

Discussion Questions

1. Have students select the excerpt from Steve's journal that explains why there are so many fights in jail. Discuss the rationale. (*"In here all you have going for you is the little surface stuff, how people look at you and what they say. And if that's all you have, then you have to protect that. Maybe that's right." People tend to concentrate on and be protective of their "rights," whether few or many. pp. 154-155*)

2. Discuss how Steve views the "real" world from jail. (*Everything seems unreal and far away. At times his movie script seems more real than his life in jail, and he wishes that all the things that are happening were just scenes in a movie. pp. 153-159*)

3. Discuss Lorelle Henry's role as witness for the prosecution. Ask students how they would evaluate the impact of her testimony. (*She was in the drugstore just before the robbery/murder and identifies James King as one of two men she heard arguing with Mr. Nesbitt about the money. pp. 161-171*)

4. Discuss how Briggs attempts to discredit Henry's testimony. (*He quizzes her about pictures of suspects she viewed and brings out that she didn't recognize King at first. He implies that the police manipulated her into identifying King, both in the pictures and in the lineup. pp. 166-170*)

Supplementary Activity

Have students reflect on Steve's statement, "They left and there was still too much Sunday left in my life." Have them write a five-senses poem about "desolation." See additional information, page 6 of this guide.

Pages 172-200

Bobo Evans testifies that he and King planned the robbery, that Steve was their lookout, and that King was responsible for firing the gun after a struggle with Nesbitt. The defense for both King and Steve challenges Bobo's credibility.

Vocabulary

sidebar (172)	prejudicial (173)	manslaughter (176)	parole (186)
concentric (199)	hurdy-gurdy (199)		

Discussion Questions

1. Discuss why Bobo Evans' appearance in court is prejudicial and the judge's reaction to defense objections. (*Bobo is dressed in a prison uniform. The judge rules against the objection because he doesn't think the uniform will make a difference. pp. 172-173*)

2. Analyze Bobo's testimony and its impact for the prosecution. (*He identifies King as someone he has known all his life and Steve as someone he met just before the robbery. He is currently in prison for selling drugs and has served time for other crimes. He says that he and King planned to rob the drugstore and enlisted Steve as the lookout. In the course of robbing the drugstore, the victim grabbed a gun and was shot in the ensuing struggle. They took the money and some cigarettes and left. He indicates no knowledge of Steve's receiving any of the money and tells the court that Steve did not give any sign when he left the drugstore. His testimony directly implicates King but leaves doubt concerning Steve's role. pp. 178-184*)

3. Analyze the defense counsel's cross-examination of Bobo Evans. (*Briggs brings out that Bobo is a dope dealer and a thief who is trying to "cop a plea" in the robbery/murder charge. Under cross-examination, Bobo tries to place the blame on King for the murder and for Bobo's "being in this mess." O'Brien elicits from Bobo the admission that what he knows about Steve's involvement is based on what King told him rather than personal knowledge. Both defense attorneys portray Bobo as vicious, manipulative, and self-interested. pp. 185-192*)

Supplementary Activities

1. Have students interpret slang: planned a getover, hit a drugstore (p. 177), everything was cool (pp. 178-179), took a hit on some crank, started a beef, came up with a chrome (p. 179), had to light him up because he was trying to muscle, dropped a dime on him, busted on a humble and went down (p. 183), cop some rocks (184).

2. Have students write a prediction. Is Steve guilty or innocent? Have a class debate.

Pages 201-214

Steve's journal reflects on his fear, his regrets, and his hopelessness.

Vocabulary

verge (203)   subdued (208)   condescendingly (209)   verify (210)
precisely (211)   access (214)

Discussion Questions

1. Discuss the strategies of both O'Brien and Briggs. (*O'Brien: separate Steve from King in the jurors' eyes. Briggs: make sure the jury connects Steve and King because Steve looks like a decent guy. p. 201*)

2. Examine how Steve feels after Bobo's testimony. (*Steve is scared, disheartened, and anxious because he thinks O'Brien believes they have lost the case. His heart is beating like crazy, he has trouble breathing, and he feels overwhelmed and crushed. pp. 201-203*)

3. Elicit student response to the words Steve would say to Jerry, "Think about all the tomorrows of your life" (p. 205). Ask how they view the tomorrows of Steve's life and of their own lives. (*Responses will vary.*)

4. Analyze the testimony of the two defense witnesses for King. (*Dorothy Moore is his cousin and testifies that he was with her the afternoon of the crime. The prosecution implies that she is lying. George Nipping testifies that King is left-handed. Briggs tries to show that Nesbitt was shot by someone who was right-handed, based on the position of the wound. The prosecution attacks his testimony through Nipping's admission that he has never seen King shoot a man. Note the weakness of both testimonies. pp. 206-214*)

Supplementary Activities

1. Have students complete the sentence, "One day in a life..." or "One mistake..."

2. Have students make a list of people they love, those who love them, and those they admire; or write a poem about the most significant person in their lives. (Refer to O'Brien's instructions to Steve on page 204.)

Pages 215-237

Steve testifies in his own defense. Mr. Sawicki testifies for the defense concerning Steve's character.

Vocabulary

infer (215)   surly (215)   soliciting (231)   compassionate (235)
depicting (235)   vouch (236)

Discussion Questions

1. Discuss O'Brien's advice to Steve, her rationale, and the implications of the "game" that she plays with him. (*She advises him to take the stand and say he is innocent because she thinks the jury wants to hear his side of the story. He must break the link between himself and King in the eyes of the jury and present himself as someone the jurors can believe in. She believes that Briggs will not have King testify in his own defense because the prosecution can prove he lied about*

knowing Bobo. The game: she places a paper cup on the table, quizzes him on several points, and turns the cup "up" for a good answer and "down" for a bad answer. Implications: she is grooming him to make the "right" answers. pp. 214-219)

2. Elicit student reaction to the definitions of truth: Steve's and the inmates'. (*Steve: what you know to be right; Inmate 1: doesn't know what truth is, prosecutor's way of looking for a way to stick you under the jail; Inmate 2: something you gave up on the street. Responses will vary. pp. 221-222)*

3. Discuss the two key prosecution points that the defense must refute. (*Bobo's testimony that Steve came out of the drugstore just before the robbery and Cruz's testimony that he was told that Steve was supposed to be the lookout. pp. 228-231)*

4. Analyze the effectiveness of Steve's testimony. (*He denies knowing about the robbery and states that he knows each of the other three alleged perpetrators of the crime only casually. Under cross-examination, he denies being in the drugstore on December 22 and says that he spent most of the day going around preparing for a school film project. He speaks firmly and confidently. pp. 223-233)*

5. Discuss the importance of Mr. Sawicki's testimony. (*He attests to Steve's honest, compassionate character and corroborates Steve's involvement in the school film project. pp. 234-237)*

Supplementary Activities

1. Have students complete the statement "Truth is..."

2. Take a secret ballot straw vote to answer the question, "Is Steve Harmon guilty or innocent?"

3. Research the turn "reasonable doubt" as a class. How is this idea important to Steve's trial?

Pages 238-253

This section features the summations of both defense attorneys. Briggs attacks Bobo Evans' character and motive. O'Brien questions the reliability of the testimony of Evans, Cruz, and King; alludes to Steve's testimony that he had nothing to do with the robbery; emphasizes Steve's character; and establishes reasonable doubt.

Vocabulary

implicates (239)	potential (242)	taint (243)	consigning (243)
indulgence (244)	elicit (245)	constitute (246)	alleged (249)
gullible (250)	acquit (253)		

Discussion Questions

1. Examine and analyze the effectiveness of Briggs' summation in King's defense. (*He alludes to Bobo's undesirable character and questions his motive in implicating King; questions the method by which Lorelle Henry picked King's picture; restates Dorothy Moore's testimony that King was with her the afternoon of the crime; refers to the "parade" of prosecution witnesses as admitted criminals; dismisses Cruz's testimony as irrelevant. Student response to the summation's effectiveness will vary. pp. 238-243)*

2. Examine and analyze the effectiveness of O'Brien's summation in Steve's defense. *(She emphasizes that the prosecution has not placed Steve in the store at the time of the robbery, has not suggested that his gun was used, nor established a conversation between Steve and anyone else about a robbery; that Lorelle Henry did not see him in the drugstore; that, though Evans said Steve was there, he stated that he did not give a signal; that only King and Evans split the money. She questions the reliability of the testimony of Evans, King, and Cruz and emphasizes Steve's character. Effectiveness: remind students that, to be effective, O'Brien's summation must establish reasonable doubt. pp. 244-253)*

Supplementary Activities

1. Have students note the body language of the following characters and ask what each communicates: Steve (p. 238), Court Officer (p. 239), Steve's mother (p. 244), two defense lawyers (p. 253).

2. Have students compare Briggs' portrayal of monsters (p. 243) with that of Steve at the beginning of the novel. Write an acrostic for MONSTER.

3. Debate: Is Steve innocent by reasonable doubt?

Pages 254-281

This section includes Petrocelli's summation for the prosecution and the denouement of the novel.

Vocabulary

contention (255)	botched (259)	moral (261)	causative (262)
bravado (266)	dialog (271)	pensive (276)	reformatory (279)

Discussion Questions

1. Summarize and analyze the effectiveness of Petrocelli's closing arguments for the State. *(She refocuses attention from the character of the witnesses to the actual crime; re-examines prosecution witnesses' testimony and points out that three witnesses placed King in the store; refers to the sale of the stolen cigarettes; presents the State's theory of a botched robbery; attacks Steve's character; asserts that all are guilty, regardless of their individual roles. Student response to effectiveness will vary. pp. 254-262)*

2. Analyze the validity of Petrocelli's statement, "Again, perhaps he [Steve] has even convinced himself that he wasn't involved" (p. 262). *(Responses will vary but students should examine Steve's testimony on the stand and his journal entries attesting to his being "not guilty.")*

3. Discuss what happens during the "waiting game" while the jury is deliberating. *(Both King and Steve are scared; the guard taunts them with references to the "pool" and what awaits them in prison; time passes slowly. Steve remembers his mother's desperate look but is consumed with thoughts of his case and the "moral decision" he made in December. He keeps editing his movie, trying to make the scenes right. pp. 265-272)*

4. Discuss the denouement. *(The jury finds King guilty and he is sentenced to 25 years to life; they find Steve innocent and he is set free. Cruz is arrested for stealing a car and sent to a reformatory. Bobo is still in jail. pp. 279-280)*

5. Analyze Steve's self-reflection. Consider his father's and O'Brien's reactions to him after the verdict. *(He makes movies of himself talking to the camera, searching for his true identity. He feels that the distance between him and his father grows bigger and bigger because his father is no longer sure who Steve is. He is troubled by the look on O'Brien's face and wonders what caused her to turn away from him. He searches for the one true image of himself. pp. 280-281)*

Supplementary Activity

Have students write poems to themselves: their alter egos or images in the mirror. Suggestions: things about themselves they like or dislike, what they really see, what they wish they could see, what they think others see, and/or what they can change.

Post-reading Discussion Questions

1. Use the Sociogram graphic on page 7 of this guide as the basis for class discussion of characters in the book. Note especially the relationship between the characters and how they influence one another.

2. Use the Herringbone graphic on page 8 of this guide as the basis for class discussion about the novel. Conclude with discussion about the outcome of the trial and what happens to each of the primary characters.

3. Discuss the thematic material of the book: self-perception, fear, guilt/innocence. Have students choose one and complete the activity on page 9 of this guide.

4. Discuss the effectiveness of Myers' interweaving of journal entries and courtroom proceedings. Ask students if and how they would change the style of writing.

5. Analyze the portrayal of life in jail. Ask students if they think this is realistic and what they think could be done to protect the inmates from attacks.

6. Have students find and discuss various references Steve makes to his participation in the crime. (See pages 49-51, 115, 128, 130, 140, 149-151.)

7. Discuss the legal terms used or alluded to throughout the novel. (perjury: lying while under oath to tell the truth; objection: reason or argument against something; sustain: to allow; overrule: to rule or decide against; summation: the final presentation of facts and arguments by the counsel for each side; plea bargain: informal practice in which the prosecuting attorney agrees to allow a defendant to plead guilty to a lesser charge in exchange for testimony against another defendant; reasonable doubt: uncertainty about guilt of a defendant; acquittal: setting free by declaring not guilty)

8. Analyze why Myers chose the name *Monster* for the novel. Ask students whether or not they view Steve as a "monster." *(Responses will vary.)*

9. Analyze Steve's perception of himself; of his guilt or innocence; of his family; of his future. *(Responses will vary.)*

10. Discuss why Steve is an unlikely candidate to be involved in a robbery/murder. *(He has a strong, loving family; he lives in a nice, clean home, with all his needs met; he is a good student who has the respect of his teachers, etc.)*

11. Why doesn't the author say whether Steve is innocent or guilty? What role must the reader take? Is it important that the reader know for certain what really happened? Why or why not?

12. Discuss the presence of peer pressure in the novel. Have students correlate with their own experiences.

Post-reading Extension Activities

Note: *The instructions for both the extension activities and the final assessment are directed toward the students. Have each student choose at least one extension activity.*

Writing

1. Rewrite the ending of the novel.

2. Write a letter from Steve to Jerry when Jerry reaches the age of 16.

3. Write an 18- to 24-line poem about a person who reminds you of Steve or about an adult who reminds you of Mr. Sawicki.

4. Write lyrics for a song that tell the story of the novel.

5. Write an "I am" poem from the persona of Steve.

   Pattern:

   Line 1: My name is...

   Line 2: I am...(three words that describe you)

   Line 3: I like...(two things such as activities, sports, food)

   Line 4: I can...(two things you do well)

   Lines 5-7: I wish I could (a) go...(b) change...(c) learn...

   Line 8: Someday I will...

6. Write a letter or poem to "The Face in the Mirror."

7. Write a review of Steve's screenplay. Would you want to watch his film? Why? What would you anticipate as its strengths and weaknesses?

8. Write about an important event in your life in script format, using Steve's as a guideline.

Art

1. Create a collage that depicts the thematic material of the novel.

2. Take photos or add a drawing such as the one on page 273 that would fit the style of artwork in the novel.

3. Design an original drawing or painting that depicts a major theme of the novel.

4. Use a video camera to create a film about your neighborhood, or based on a short script of a personal event, or re-enact a scene from Steve's screenplay.

Music

1. Select a cassette or CD of music that fits the mood of one particular journal entry in the novel. Play the music in the background as you read that entry.

2. Compose a ballad that tells the story of Steve's search for himself.

Drama

Use Steve's script to act out a scene from the book

Social Studies

Draw a map of the section of New York City depicted in the novel. Indicate locations for various events.

Language Study

Develop a glossary of legal words, film terms, or slang words used in the novel.

Assessment for *Monster*

Assessment is an ongoing process. The following eight items can be completed during the novel study. Once finished, the student and teacher will check the work. Points may be added to indicate the level of understanding.

Name _____ Date _____

Student   **Teacher**

_____   _____   1. Correct any quizzes or tests taken over the novel.

_____   _____   2. Pretend you are a juror for Steve's court case. What argument would you make for or against Steve's innocence behind closed doors? Write a persuasive essay, outlining each piece of evidence for your argument.

_____   _____   3. Write two review questions about the novel, and then use these questions as the class conducts an oral review.

_____   _____   4. Write a two-line description of one of the characters but omit the name. Exchange with a partner and identify the character s/he has described.

_____   _____   5. List the primary characters from the book. Choose and write one noun that is synonymous with that character; for example, victim, victimizer, etc.

_____   _____   6. What are some of society's stereotypes about lawyers? Write a short essay explaining how *Monster* reinforced or challenged those stereotypes.

_____   _____   7. Share your extension project with the class on the assigned day.

_____   _____   8. Write a review of the book using at least ten of the vocabulary words you learned from the novel.

Glossary

Pages 1-58

1. dispensary (2): hospital, infirmary, sick bay

2. grainy (3): rough, unrefined; texture resembling wood grain

3. obscene (7): indecent, offensive

4. felony (12): crime more serious than misdemeanor

5. mentor (19): advisor, teacher, guide, counselor

6. safeguard (21): protection, defense

7. merits (21): goodness, worth, value; something that deserves praise or reward

8. infringing (21): transgressing; breaking

9. conspiracy (23): intrigue, plot; act of combining for an evil purpose

10. impede (23): hinder, obstruct

11. redress (26): act of setting right; relief, restitution

12. lynch (26): kill; put to death without lawful trial; hanging by a mob

13. grandiose (27): imposing, pretentious; planned on a great scale

14. articulate (28): well-spoken, eloquent, fluent

15. inventory (31): make a listing of goods

16. careens (42): tilts, tips; leans to one side

17. tentative (42): hesitant, not definite; done as a trial; experimental

18. drawl (50): to speak with drawn-out vowels

19. pertinent (55): to the point; appropriate

20. silhouetted (57): an object outlined against the light

Pages 59-126

1. affidavit (66): written statement or oath

2. pans (67): to move a motion picture or television camera either vertically or horizontally to take in a larger scene or to follow a moving object

3. grotesque (68): distorted; absurd

---

4. pessimist (73): one who has the tendency to see the worst side of things

5. lethal (73): deadly; fatal

6. grimaces (73): to make distorted, wry faces

7. perpetrator (74): one who commits offense or crime

8. proposition (85): statement or assertion; suggestion of terms

9. juvenile (86): young person, child

10. civil (88): polite, courteous

11. judicial (97): of judges; having to do with a law court or the administration of justice

12. apprehended (102): taken hold of; seized by authority

13. ruffled (107): annoyed, put out

14. hexagon (110): figure with six sides

15. cope (111): contend, deal with

16. cacophony (117): disagreeable sound; discord of sounds

17. ghetto (120): part of a city where members of a minority group live, especially because of social, economic, or legal pressure

18. dismay (121): consternation; horrified amazement

19. glowers (123): scowls; stares angrily or fiercely

20. precinct (124): division of a city as relates to policing and voting

Pages 127-200

1. arcs (130): parts of a circle or other curve

2. montage (131): rapid succession of different images, etc. in a film; composite of juxtaposed elements

3. premises (131): a house or building with its grounds

4. perimeter (133): outer boundary of a figure

5. traversed (135): crossed; gone through or over

6. trapezius (135): each of a pair of large, flat, triangular muscles of the back, the neck, and the upper part of the back and shoulders, together forming a somewhat diamond-shaped figure

7. wrenched (147): twisted; seized forcibly

8. mosaic (151): picture or pattern made by arranging small bits of colored stone, glass, etc.

9. whist (154): card game

10. diminutive (161): very small

11. sidebar (legal term) (172): approach of court officials to side of judge's bench for private conference

12. prejudicial (173): detrimental; indicating unwarranted judgment

13. manslaughter (176): killing of a human being unlawfully but without deliberate intent or under strong provocation

14. parole (186): early release of prisoner on the condition of good behavior

15. concentric (199): having a common center

16. hurdy-gurdy (199): portable hand-organ; barrel-organ

Pages 201-237

1. verge (203): edge, brink

2. subdued (208): overcome; tamed; toned down

3. condescendingly (209): patronizingly, haughtily

4. verify (210): prove or confirm the truth of

5. precisely (211): exactly; carefully observed

6. access (214): admission; entrance; liberty to approach

7. infer (215): deduce by reasoning; conclude

8. surly (215): unfriendly, ill-tempered

9. soliciting (231): seeking; requesting; enticing, urging

10. compassionate (235): filled with pity and sympathy

11. depicting (235): giving a picture of

12. vouch (236): make oneself responsible for; guarantee

Pages 239-281

1. implicates (239): involves; entangles

2. potential (242): latent ability; capacity for use or development

3. taint (243): stain slightly; corrupt

4. consigning (243): committing or handing over to

5. indulgence (244): lenience, tolerance, understanding

6. elicit (245): draw out

7. constitute (246): set up, establish; give form to

8. alleged (249): brought forward as an argument without proof; purported

9. gullible (250): easily deceived; naive

10. acquit (253): declare not guilty

11. contention (255): conflict, disruption, dissension

12. botched (259): patched or put together clumsily; bungled

13. moral (261): good in character; virtuous, honest, exemplary [note: moral tightrope (261), moral hairs (262), moral decision (262)]

14. causative (262): functioning as an agent or cause

15. bravado (266): boastful display of boldness; swagger

16. dialog (271): conversation between two or more

17. pensive (276): thoughtful with sadness; wistful

18. reformatory (270): institution for reforming juvenile offenders